Midnight Dance
of the
Snowshoe Hare

POEMS OF ALASKA

NANCY WHITE CARLSTROM

ILLUSTRATED BY KEN KUROI

PHILOMEL BOOKS NEW YORK

AUTHOR'S NOTE

Outside, the trees are heavy with snow and the valley below lies shrouded in ice fog. Tonight's full moon will only add to the magic. Will the Snowshoe Hare, dressed in white, dance in the forest clearing?

I love seeing the wildlife around our house. Even when I don't see the animals, I know they are here by their tracks or the way they nibble the willows. I look up when I hear the gurgling cry of the Raven. I stop and listen to the drumming of the Grouse, or the song of the hardy Chickadee. Sometimes I am lucky enough to hear the bell-like tones of the Boreal Owl in the middle of the night.

But this collection is not about the ice and snow. It is about Alaska's other seasons: a short spring and fall, and glorious summer—a time of no darkness and great energy. One cannot see stars in the sky from the first week of May until the second week of August.

Moose raid the garden, and Red Squirrels frolic high in the black spruce. Once I saw a Wolf lope off through the flickering green of sun-streaked trees. Another time I watched as a Spruce Grouse fanned his feathers and danced. As I remember, I say, "Ahh—Alaska! The Great Land!"

And yet, even in the warm, long, light days of summer, winter is never far away. Many of these poems and much of the art feature Snowshoe Hare, who seem well suited for living in this place all year long. Their large feet take them lightly over the snow, and changing coats of color provide camouflage. I see their tracks in the light of day but can only imagine their midnight dance.

Midnight Dance of the Snowshoe Hare
(SUMMER SOLSTICE)

When the sun is high
And the light shines
Lavender and pink
On the mountains
The Snowshoe Hare
Gather in the clearing.

They come out of their hiding
Behind the hills,
Where they have waited and watched,
Watched and waited,
All the year 'round.

They come hopping on silent paws
And carry their own music.

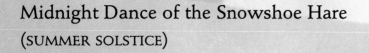

And in the golden light,
The trees—birch, aspen, and larch,
Outlined in flame,
Lean forward to whisper.

The Snowshoe Hare form a circle.
It is the longest day of the year.

Magic crackles in the warm, full air.

They take out their songs, one by one,
And give them up to the light of the sun.

For the moment, the Snowshoe Hare are safe.
They know their Joys and call them by name.

Chickadee-dee-dee

Chickadee-dee-dee,
Chickadee-dee-dee,

Your song flits from branch to branch.

We sit in the warm spot
your music makes.

Chickadee-dee-dee,
Chickadee-dee-dee,

Summer   winter
Grass   snow

Your music fills the air,
while joy gets caught in our throats.

We wish we could sing,
But sometimes when our feet leap
And we leave the earth behind,
We become a song.

Ode to Nibbling

Willow
Cottonwood
Alder
Aspen
Larch

Nibbling Nibbling
In the light and dark.

Winter
Spring breakup
Summer
Autumn chill

Nibbling Nibbling
Till we get our fill.

Twigs and
Needles
Tenderbuds
And bark

Nibbling Nibbling
In the light and dark.

Young Wolf

Young Wolf,
You wear your wildness well
From tilt of head
To droop of tail.
It stretches taut
Over your haunches
And rides your shadow
Through the summer woods.

Sun at the Top of the World

Sun, Sun,
Where do you live in summer?

I live in my house at the top of the world,
At the top of the world in summer.

Sun, Sun,
What do you see at the top of the world?
What do you see in summer?

I see wide-open space
Where the sea and the land keep walking.
I see sky-stretching blue
Like a giant sealskin,
And clouds with a polar bear ruff.

Sun, Sun,
What do you smell at the top of the world?
What do you smell in summer?

I smell the sea that winter lets go
With the wind of a thousand summers.
I smell the willows hugging the tundra,
And poppies blowing with color.

Sun, Sun,
What do you hear at the top of the world?
What do you hear in summer?

I hear the tales that the old men tell
Of hunting the Whale and the Caribou.
I hear the steps of the dancing women,
And games that the children play.
I hear the Arctic Loon laugh as he asks,
"Where have you been all winter?"

Sun, Sun,
How do you feel at the top of the world?
How do you feel in summer?

I feel so alive
Where I live in my house
At the top of the world in summer
That I wish
I could stay all winter.

Song of the Aspen Aunties

Swaying together in rustling skirts
The Aspen Aunties are singing their song
Under midnight sun when the wind goes walking
Whispering
Whispering
All night long.

Where is the darknesss?
Where has it gone?
Why does the day
Go on and on?

Swaying together in rustling skirts
The Aspen Aunties are dancing their song
With long hair flying, the Aunties are sighing
Whispering
Whispering
All night long.

Where is the darkness?
Where has it gone?
Why does the day
Go on and on?

Under midnight sun when the wind goes walking
Whispering
Whispering
Until the dawn.

Song of the Wise Grandfather

Many moons ago
When I was as young
As new grass
I walked through
The Valley of Death.

In the shadow
Of the Great Horned Owl
I stood frozen.

By the talons
Of the Great Horned Owl
I was carried
On the wings of Fear.

I am alive today
Because of the light
The light of the northern sky
Aurora Borealis.

In the surprise
Of the Great Horned Owl
I was dropped.

The moon hid
Behind a cloud
And I was cradled
In fresh snow.
That was long ago, my grandson.

It was the beginning of wisdom for me.
Now I pass it on to you.

Friends of the Forest

Meadow Voles Meadow Mice
We see you eating
Day and night.

You stay so small
But your children number
More than the stars
More than ours.
We bless you under the sun.

Red Squirrel Red Squirrel
We don't always like the spruce cones
you drop on our heads.

But your scolding chatter
Is a welcome sound.
The times it has warned us
Of danger are many.
We thank you under the sun.

Grouse Grouse
Spruce and Tuffed
Rock and Willow Ptarmigan.

You have your own drumming
Your own dance.
But what we admire most
Is the way you take care of your children.

If we have disturbed an egg
Or caused you fright,
Forgive us under the sun.

May we be one in peace.
Summer and winter
Circle the seasons

Now and forever. Amen.

When Night Is Bright Like Day

In summer
When night is bright like day
The stars we see
Are wildflowers.

But if we close our eyes
We see winter sky
And stars shining in darkness.

In summer
When night is bright like day
The sun we see
Cuts a path to the river.

But if we close our eyes
We see winter sun
Struggling to sit up
Above the horizon.

In summer
When night is bright like day
The river we see
Rolls over with boats and fish.

But if we close our eyes
We see winter river
Solid ribbon of ice
Winding through silence.

In summer
When night is bright like day
The trees we see
Wear sunshine and Red Squirrels.

But if we close our eyes
We see winter trees
Asleep in snow
Kissed by the moon.

In summer
When night is bright like day
We think the midnight sun
Will last forever.

But if we close our eyes
We see winter light
Dim, short-lived
And weaving its own magic.

Grandma River

Grandma River,
Rolling through town
Shining out from under the bridge
Of summer shade

Tell us what you see in the country
Where the Wolf family comes to you
For an evening drink;

Where the Beaver
Slaps your bank
And chinks his lodge with your cool-gray mud;

Where the Fox
Brushes green leaves
With its red tail
Like an artist;

And the tiny Vole
Stuffs cheeks with summer seeds.

Tell us what it is like
Moving swiftly through all that wildness,
Where the trapper's cabin stands empty,
Waiting for winter.

Do you stop to sing when the animals dance
In the clearing at the bend in your arm?

Grandma River,
Tell us your story.
Sing us your song.

Grandfather, Can I Be Friends with a Sled Dog?

Sled Dog,
We have watched you
Through the summer trees.
We have seen you
Nap in the sun
Dreaming of snow.

We have crouched low
As you jumped on top
Of your box
Sniffing the air.

Do you smell winter?

Sled Dog,
My grandson wants to like you.
But still
When you
Tug at your chain
And howl
You make us shiver
More than winter.

But Grandfather, I Like Wearing Two Colors.

Listen, my grandson, and look.

See how the birch wear yellow,
And aspen autumn gold.
Wildrose leaves are bronze,
Their rosehips plump.
Lowbush cranberries glow
Ruby red on the forest floor.

The purple pink is all used up
In fireweed gone to seed;
Its pods are soft,
More fluff than a newborn Hare.
The fields wear Sandhill Cranes.
They dot the land in black and tan.

We wear our brown with worry now
And watch the sky for snow.
O that we could slip quickly into white
Like a coat and not know fear.

Be careful, my grandson. Be careful.

Winter Is Coming

Children, Children,
Winter is coming.

Pick the berries that glow in the forest
Stack the wood, and rake the yard
Gather the lettuce, the dill, the zucchini
Cut the flowers, the flowers, the flowers
Fill all the jars with leftover summer.

Red Squirrel, Red Squirrel,
Winter is coming.

See how the birch and aspen stand golden
Carry the cones that the black spruce gives
Build your nest now, behind the old woodpile
Say to the world, "These are my cones.
This is my home. I am ready for winter."

Beaver, Beaver,
Winter is coming.

Gnaw on the willows. Your lodge must be built.
Pack the cracks tightly with silt and mud plaster
Such a fast worker, you store up some extra
Mounding the branches for winter's fine dining
A nearby supply for the days of long darkness.

River, River,
Winter is coming.

Give of your Grayling, Whitefish, and Salmon
Give of your plenty before you are frozen
Sing in the sunlight and wink in your running
As days shorten quickly, for winter is coming
Soon you will freeze and be silent till spring.

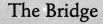

The Bridge

We want to walk across the bridge
But we don't know if it is strong enough.
Then a Moose family trudges by.
The bridge will not break.

We want to walk across the bridge
But we don't know how long it will take.
Then many Voles skitter by.
It doesn't take long at all.

We want to walk across the bridge
But we don't know if it is safe.
Then five Caribou with Ravens
    riding on their antlers click by.
It will be okay.

We want to walk across the bridge
     and be with you,
But we don't know what you will call us.
Then we hear you naming the animals.
We think you will call us friends.

We want to walk across the bridge
But we don't know if you will understand us.
Then we hear you sing.
Arctic Loons listen,
Snowy Owls swoop from the sky.
We all will learn new songs.

We want to walk across the bridge
But still we are afraid to go.
Then you come halfway to meet us.
We walk across the bridge together.

Raven Cries River

Snowshoe Hare, brown on white,
Sled Dog sniffing winter
Grouse family frantic
Scatters leaves like wind
Red Squirrel storing summer.
Gangly Moose
Dangling broccoli
Dancing purple cabbage.

And Raven,
Bold rascal Raven
Cries River
Rippling
  Rippling
    Autumn gold.

Snowshoe Hare, white on white,
Sled Dog pulling moonlight
Grouse family hiding
Burrows snow like nest
Red Squirrel tunnels woodpile.
Gangly Moose
Dangling branches
Browsing full on willow.

And Raven,
Bold rascal Raven
Cries River
   Slicing
      Stillness
         Winter ice.

Snowshoe Hare, white on light,
Sled Dog dreaming big race
Grouse family comic
Roosting tree like joke
Red Squirrel carries sunshine.
Gangly Moose
Dangling new buds
Stamping mud from snowmelt.

And Raven,
Bold rascal Raven
Cries River
  Ice chunks crashing
    Water rushing
      Spring breakup!

Snowshoe Hare, brown on brown,
Sled Dog whining winter
Grouse family growing
Chicks and chicks and chicks
Red Squirrel jumping treetops.
Gangly Moose
Dangling green leaves
Feasting fine on garden.

And Raven,
Bold rascal Raven
Cries River
   Rippling
     Rippling
       Summer free.

For Sue Sherif and Nanette Stevenson—N.W.C.

To my little friends in Alaska—K.K.

Library of Congress Cataloging-in-Publication Data
Carlstrom, Nancy White. Midnight dance of the snowshoe hare / Nancy White Carlstrom;
[illustrated by] Ken Kuroi.   p.   cm.   Summary: Poems about Alaska's beautiful but
brief spring, summer and fall seasons, which provide a short respite from the cold,
dark winter.   1. Natural history—Alaska—Juvenile poetry.   2. Children's poetry, American.
3. Nature—Juvenile poetry.   [1. Nature—Poetry.   2. Alaska—Poetry.   3. American poetry.]
I. Kuroi, Ken, 1947–   ill.   II. Title.   PS3553.A7355M5   1998   811'.54—dc20
95-44606   CIP   AC   ISBN 0-399-22746-6
10 9 8 7 6 5 4 3 2 1   First Impression